A little wonder goes a long way.

PBS KIDS

Do It Myself COOKBOOK

Nothing Sharp, Nothing Hot!

downtown bookworks

downtown 🏢 bookworks

Copyright © 2015 Downtown Bookworks Inc.
All rights reserved. No part of this book may be reproduced in any form or
by any means without prior written permission from the publisher.

Recipes by Laurie Goldrich Wolf
Photographs by Bruce Wolf
How-to Illustrations by Matt Shay/Shay Design
Cover and introduction photos by Ellen Wallop

Special thanks to our wonderful model chefs:
Apple Diamond, Ava Gordon, Kal Katz, Nathanael Katz, Emma Loyim,
Hannah Loyim, Jahmal Marajah

Designed by Georgia Rucker Design
Typeset in Museo Rounded and PBS Headline

Printed in China
May 2016

ISBN 9781941367018

10 9 8 7 6 5 4 3 2

Downtown Bookworks Inc.
265 Canal Street
New York, NY 10013

www.downtownbookworks.com

A little wonder goes a long way.

PBS KIDS

Do It Myself COOKBOOK

by Laurie Goldrich Wolf

PHOTOGRAPHS BY BRUCE WOLF · ILLUSTRATIONS BY MATT SHAY

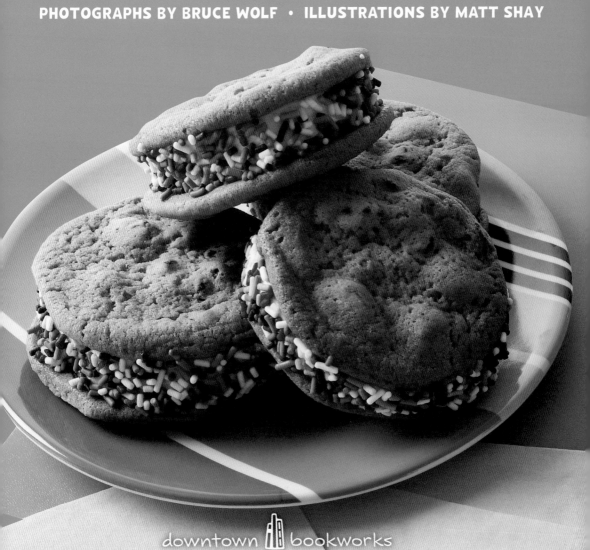

downtown bookworks

CONTENTS

INTRODUCTION 4

 SANDWICHES

SNACKS

SALADS, DRESSINGS, & DIPS

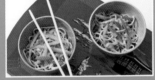

DESSERTS

DRINKS

Hey there, grown-ups!

Thank you for buying the *PBS KIDS Do It Myself Cookbook* for the smaller chefs in your life. Before you turn the show over to any young foodies, please read the following words of wisdom regarding kitchen safety and setup, as well as suggestions for how best to use this book.

ALL SMALL CHEFS MUST:

- Wash hands with soap and warm water.
- Tie back long hair.

ALL GROWN-UPS IN CHARGE SHOULD:

- Clear a work space. (For easy cleanup, tape newspaper or kraft paper over the workspace before you begin.) Find a chair that is a good height for your child so that he or she can pour, mix, and measure comfortably.
- Provide an apron, if you have one, and a kitchen towel for chefs to wipe their hands.
- Wash all fresh fruits and vegetables thoroughly before putting them out.
- Once the workspace, tools, and ingredients have been set up, stay close by. Although this book is designed to enable kids to work independently, young children still require supervision.
- When a recipe calls for using kids' scissors, make sure the scissors are clean. If they aren't, you can chop up the herbs with kitchen shears or a knife as part of the recipe prep.

More than great food...

Cooking offers lots of opportunities for learning and is a fun way to encourage independence. Every recipe in this book requires counting, measuring, and following sequential directions— all important skills for children to master. Picky eaters are also more likely to try new foods if they're preparing a meal themselves. Best of all, being able to eat and serve something that they've made will give your child a terrific sense of accomplishment. Enjoy!

CHOOSING A RECIPE

- Become familiar with the tools and ingredients lists in the book. You will see a definite pattern of repeated tools (plastic knives, cutting boards, big bowls, wooden spoons, etc.) and kid-friendly foods (berries, cheese, cold cuts, pasta, crackers, cookies, etc.). Most of these ingredients are pantry or refrigerator staples.

- At the back of the book, you will find an ingredients index. If you have sliced turkey you'd like to use up, strawberries that would be most delicious eaten TODAY, or a child who can't ever eat enough corn, this ingredients index will be the most efficient way to approach the question, "What shall we make?"

- Many of these recipes were designed for turning leftovers into yummy new dishes. Consider saving recipes that call for cooked chicken breasts or fried chicken for days when you already have them on hand.

- Some recipes call for salad dressing. We've provided basic recipes for salad dressings, but if you have others you prefer, feel free to use them.

- The extent of the grown-up preparation in the book is minimal; not much more than cooking (or pulling out leftover) pasta, hard-boiling eggs, coring and slicing apples, or toasting bread. When putting out liquid ingredients such as milk or water, you can decide whether a milk carton or a pitcher of water goes on the workspace with an empty measuring cup or whether you will be doing the measuring.

  - To cut down on grown-up prep, ingredients such as grated carrots or shredded cheese may be purchased in their bagged form. Of course, the correct amount can always be grated or shredded by the grown-up in charge.

    - Most of the recipes serve 1 or 2 kids. If they serve more, we've let you know.

LIST OF PANTRY ITEMS USED IN THIS BOOK

STAPLES: almond butter, bagels (cinnamon swirl, mini), bread (cinnamon raisin, white, whole wheat), cereal (crisped rice, graham cracker, honey nut O's, rice biscuit), chocolate chips, chocolate frosting, chopped dates, cookies, crackers, dried apricots, dried cranberries, flour tortillas, golden raisins, graham crackers, granola, hard corn taco shells, honey, ice cream cones, marshmallow creme, pasta, peanut butter, pita (mini, regular), rice, salsa, shredded coconut, small pretzels, sprinkles, super fine sugar, vanilla instant pudding mix, vanilla wafers

CANNED GOODS: black beans, corn, crushed pineapple, garbanzo beans (chickpeas), light red kidney beans, peas, pitted black olives, roasted peppers, tuna

SPICES AND SEASONINGS: Asian sesame oil, black pepper, cilantro, dry mustard, fresh dill, fresh parsley, garlic powder, mint leaves, olive oil, paprika, red wine vinegar, salt, soy sauce, Worcestershire sauce

FRESH FRUITS AND VEGETABLES: apples, avocados, bananas, blueberries, cucumbers, fresh peppers, grated carrots, lettuce, peaches, pears, potatoes, raspberries, scallions, seedless grapes, strawberries, tomatoes

LIST OF FRIDGE ITEMS USED IN THIS BOOK

STAPLES: blue cheese, buttermilk, Cheddar cheese, chicken breast, chocolate syrup, cold cuts (ham, roast beef, turkey), cranberry sauce, cream cheese, frozen corn, frozen pound cake, hard-boiled eggs, hummus, ice cream, ketchup, lemon juice, mayonnaise, milk, mozzarella cheese, Muenster cheese, mustard (Dijon, yellow), orange juice, Parmesan cheese, pesto, pickle relish, pickles, pineapple juice, pink lemonade, plain and flavored yogurts, salad dressings, seltzer, shrimp, sour cream, strawberry jam, strawberry syrup, Swiss cheese, whipped cream, white grape juice

Peanut Butter, Banana, Strawberry, and Coconut on Cinnamon Raisin Bread

TOOLS

- **Cutting board**
- **1 tablespoon** — 1 tbsp
- **Spreader**
- **Plastic knife**

INGREDIENTS

- **3 slices cinnamon raisin bread**
- **2 tablespoons peanut butter**
- **1 small banana**
- **1 tablespoon honey**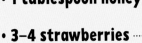
- **3–4 strawberries**
- **2 tablespoons shredded coconut**

MIX IT UP: Instead of peanut butter, you can also make this stackable sandwich with almond butter or a thin layer of cream cheese.

1. Place 1 slice of bread on a cutting board. Put 2 tablespoons of peanut butter on the bread. Using a spreader, smooth the peanut butter to the edges of the bread.

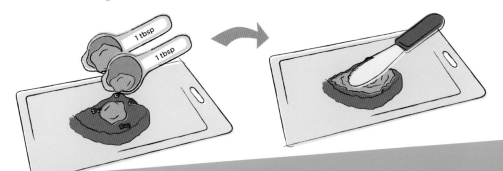

TURN PAGE

CONTINUED
Peanut Butter, Banana, Strawberry, and Coconut on Cinnamon Raisin Bread

2. Peel the banana. On the cutting board, use a plastic knife to cut the banana into thin slices. Place the banana slices on the peanut butter—they'll stick nicely.

3. Place the next piece of bread on top of the banana slices. Measure 1 tablespoon of honey, then drizzle the honey over the top slice of bread. Use the spreader to cover the whole slice of bread with the honey.

4. On the cutting board, use a plastic knife to cut the strawberries into thin slices. Lay the strawberry slices on top of the honey.

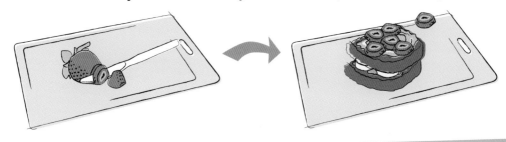

5. Sprinkle 2 tablespoons of coconut over the strawberry slices.

6. Place the last slice of bread on top of the strawberries and coconut. Gently cut with the plastic knife, or eat without cutting. This sandwich can be a little messy, but it tastes wonderful!

Hard-boiled Egg, Apple, and Chicken Salad on Crispy Crackers

TOOLS

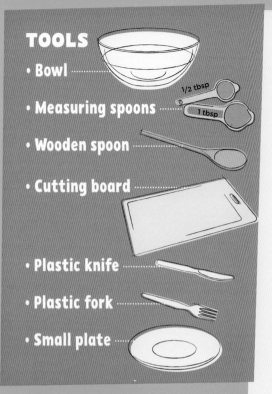

- Bowl
- Measuring spoons
- Wooden spoon
- Cutting board
- Plastic knife
- Plastic fork
- Small plate

INGREDIENTS

- 2 tablespoons mayonnaise
- ½ tablespoon mustard
- 2 tablespoons grated carrots
- 1 scallion
- 1 cooked chicken breast
- Salt
- 1 hard-boiled egg
- 6 pieces long crackers, crispbread, or flatbread
- 2 apple quarters

GROWN-UP PREP: 2 tablespoons grated carrot; 1 cooked chicken breast; 1 hard-boiled egg, peeled; 1 apple, cored and quartered

1. Put 2 tablespoons of mayonnaise and ½ tablespoon of mustard into a bowl. Using a wooden spoon, stir them together. Mix in 2 tablespoons of grated carrots.

TURN PAGE

CONTINUED
Hard-boiled Egg, Apple, and Chicken Salad on Crispy Crackers

2. On the cutting board, use the plastic knife to slice a scallion into very thin slices. Add the scallion slices to the bowl. Stir to mix.

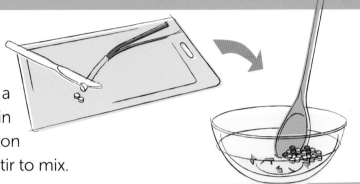

3. On the cutting board, use the plastic knife and fork to cut the chicken breast into small pieces. (If that's too hard, shred the meat with your hands.)

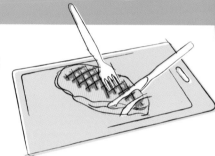

4. Put the chicken pieces into the bowl. Add a pinch of salt. Mix again.

5. On a cutting board, use a plastic knife to cut the hard-boiled egg into thin slices.

6. Place the first piece of cracker on the cutting board. Lay 2–3 egg slices on the cracker. Place the remaining slices on a plate.

7. On the cutting board, use the plastic knife to cut the 2 apple quarters into thin slices.

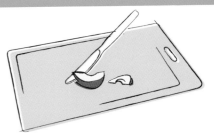

8. Lay the apple slices on top of the egg slices. Place a second piece of cracker on top of the apple slices.

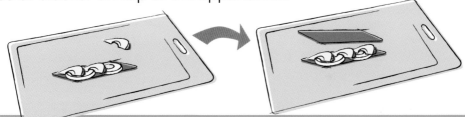

9. Using the wooden spoon, gently spread the chicken salad to the edges of the cracker. Top with a third cracker. Make another sandwich with the remaining ingredients.

Cream Cheese, Strawberry, and Pineapple Quesadilla

TOOLS

- Cutting board
- 1 tablespoon
- Plastic knife
- ⅓ measuring cup

INGREDIENTS

- 3 6-inch flour tortillas
- 2 tablespoons cream cheese at room temperature
- 5 tablespoons crushed pineapple
- 2 tablespoons strawberry jam
- 4 medium strawberries

GROWN-UP PREP:
1 can crushed pineapple, opened and drained into a bowl

1. Place 1 tortilla on a cutting board. Put 2 tablespoons of cream cheese on the tortilla. Using a plastic knife, spread the cream cheese evenly over the tortilla.

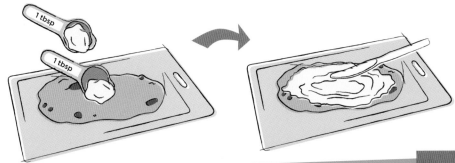

TURN PAGE

CONTINUED
Cream Cheese, Strawberry, and Pineapple Quesadilla

2. Put ⅓ cup of crushed pineapple on top of the cream cheese. Use the plastic knife to spread the pineapple to the edges of the tortilla.

3. Place a second tortilla on top of the pineapple.

4. Add 2 tablespoons of strawberry jam. Using the plastic knife, spread the jam to the edges of the tortilla.

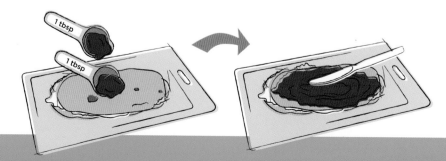

5. On the cutting board, use the plastic knife to thinly slice the strawberries. Place the strawberry slices on top of the jam.

6. Cover with the third tortilla. Using the plastic knife, cut the quesadilla into wedges.

Honey, Berries, and Almond Butter on Graham Crackers

TOOLS

- Cutting board
- Measuring spoons
- Butter knife

INGREDIENTS

- 2 double graham crackers
- 2 tablespoons almond butter
- 12 raspberries
- 1 tablespoon honey

MIX IT UP: This sandwich is also tasty with blueberries or blackberries.

1. Over a cutting board, break 1 double graham cracker in half along the scored line. Now, you have 2 square crackers.

2. Put 1 tablespoon of almond butter on each cracker. Using a butter knife, spread the almond butter to the edges.

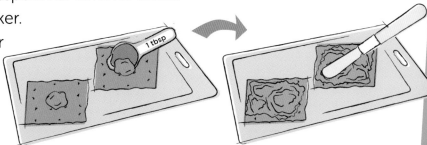

3. Place 6 raspberries on top of the almond butter on each cracker.

4. Drizzle ½ tablespoon of honey over the raspberries on one of the crackers. Then, drizzle ½ tablespoon of honey over the other cracker.

5. Break the remaining graham cracker in half along the scored line to make 2 square crackers. Place the crackers on top of the raspberries and honey. Enjoy!

Egg Salad with Red and Yellow Peppers on Flower Toast

TOOLS

- Medium bowl
- Potato masher
- 1 tablespoon
- Wooden spoon
- Cutting board
- Plastic knife
- Flower-shaped cookie cutter

INGREDIENTS

- 2 hard-boiled eggs
- 3 tablespoons mayonnaise
- Salt
- Black pepper
- $\frac{1}{2}$ red pepper
- $\frac{1}{2}$ yellow pepper
- 2 slices white bread, toasted

GROWN-UP PREP: 2 hard-boiled eggs, peeled; 2 slices white bread, toasted

1. Put 2 hard-boiled eggs in a bowl. Using a potato masher, press down on the eggs. Mash them until the eggs are broken into small pieces.

2. Add 3 tablespoons of mayonnaise to the mashed eggs. Add a pinch of salt and a few grinds of black pepper. Using a wooden spoon, stir everything together.

3. On a cutting board, use a plastic knife to cut the red and yellow peppers into the skinniest strips you can. They don't all have to be the same size. Set the pepper strips aside.

4. Press a cookie cutter into a piece of toast to make a flower shape. Repeat on the second piece of toast.

5. Put half the egg salad on each piece of toast. Using the plastic knife, spread the egg salad evenly around the toast. Lay the red and yellow pepper slices on top of the egg salad.

Ham, Hard-boiled Egg, and Olives on Whole Wheat

TOOLS

- Cutting board
- ½ tablespoon
- Butter knife
- Plastic knife

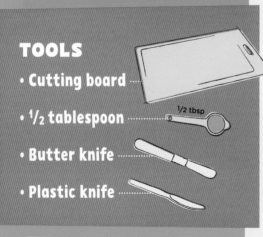

1/2 tbsp

INGREDIENTS

- 1 slice whole wheat bread
- ½ tablespoon mayonnaise
- 2 slices baked or boiled ham
- 1 hard-boiled egg
- 4 pitted black olives

GROWN-UP PREP: 1 hard-boiled egg, peeled; 1 can pitted black olives, opened, drained, and placed in a small bowl

1. Place the bread on a cutting board. Put ½ tablespoon of mayonnaise on the bread. Using a butter knife, spread the mayonnaise to the edges of the bread.

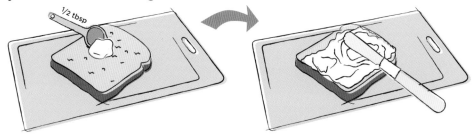

2. Place 2 slices of ham on top of the mayonnaise.

3. On a cutting board, use a plastic knife to cut the egg into thin slices. Place the egg slices on top of the ham.

4. On the cutting board, use the plastic knife to cut the olives into thin slices. Place the olive slices on top of the egg slices. Cut the sandwich in quarters with a plastic knife or eat it whole.

Turkey, Cheese, and Roasted Pepper Roll-ups

TOOLS

- Cutting board
- Paper towels
- Plastic knife
- Toothpicks

INGREDIENTS

- 1 6-inch flour tortilla
- 2 slices roast turkey
- 2 slices Cheddar cheese
- 1 whole roasted pepper from a jar

MIX IT UP: Sliced roll-ups make pretty pinwheels, especially when you use colorful ingredients. Try with ham or another deli meat and different types of cheese. Lettuce, cabbage, avocado, or shredded carrots can be added to the mix too!

1. Put a tortilla on the cutting board. Place 2 slices of turkey on the tortilla, covering up as much tortilla as possible.

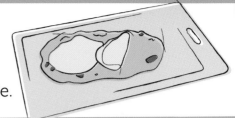

2. Place 2 slices of Cheddar cheese on the turkey. Set aside the tortilla.

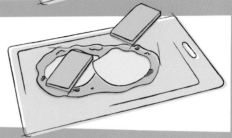

3. Place the roasted pepper on a paper towel and drain off any oil or liquid. On the cutting board, use a plastic knife to thinly slice the roasted pepper. Lay the pepper slices on top of the Cheddar cheese.

4. Roll up the tortilla, gently pressing it together as you roll so it will stay closed.

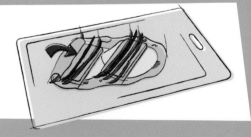

5. Using the plastic knife, slice the roll into 1-inch pieces. Push a toothpick into each roll to keep it closed.

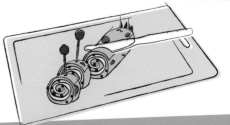

Shrimp Tacos with Avocado and Corn

TOOLS

- Cutting board
- Plastic knife
- Medium bowl
- Measuring spoons — 1/2 tbsp, 1 tbsp
- Wooden spoon

INGREDIENTS

- 6 small cooked shrimp
- 3 tablespoons canned or cooked corn
- 1/2 avocado
- 1/2 tablespoon lemon juice
- 2 tablespoons yogurt salsa dressing (see page 70)
- 2 hard corn taco shells

GROWN-UP PREP: avocado, pitted and peeled; canned corn, opened and drained into a small bowl, or fresh corn, cut off the cob into a small bowl

1. On a cutting board, use a plastic knife to cut 6 shrimp into small pieces. Put the shrimp in the bowl.

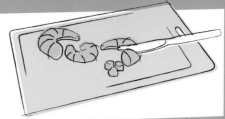

2. Add 3 tablespoons of corn to the bowl. Using a wooden spoon, mix the shrimp and corn.

3. On the cutting board, use a plastic knife to cut the avocado into small pieces. Add the avocado and ½ tablespoon of lemon juice to the bowl. Stir gently.

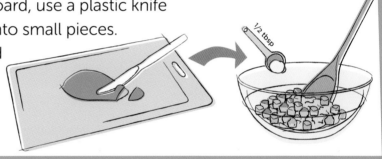

4. Add 2 tablespoons of yogurt salsa dressing to the bowl. Gently stir the ingredients together.

5. Spoon the shrimp mixture into the taco shells.

Cheddar, Turkey, and Cucumber Slices on Crackers

TOOLS

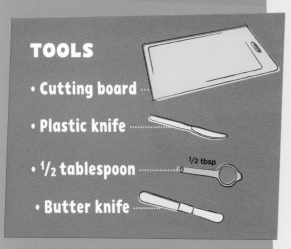

- Cutting board
- Plastic knife
- ½ tablespoon   1/2 tbsp
- Butter knife

INGREDIENTS

- 4 round, buttery crackers
- 2 slices Cheddar cheese
- 2 slices turkey
- 1 small cucumber, washed

- 1 tablespoon mayonnaise

MIX IT UP: Have you ever eaten a radish? Here's your chance! Instead of cucumber slices, use thinly sliced radishes.

1. Put 2 crackers on the cutting board. Place 1 slice of Cheddar cheese on each cracker. Fold a slice of turkey and place it on top of the Cheddar cheese. (If the turkey slices are too big, tear them in half before folding them.)

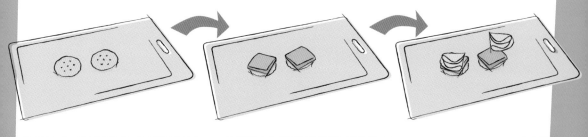

2. On the cutting board, use a plastic knife to cut 6 thin cucumber slices. Pile 3 thin slices of cucumber on each turkey-covered cracker.

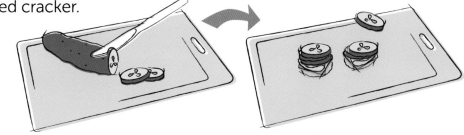

3. Using a butter knife, spread ½ tablespoon of mayonnaise on top of the 2 remaining crackers.

½ tbsp

4. Top each cracker sandwich with a mayonnaise-covered cracker.

Cheddar, Ham, and Raisins on Whole Wheat Hearts

TOOLS

- Cutting board
- 1 tablespoon
- 3- or 4-inch heart-shaped cookie cutter

INGREDIENTS

- 4 slices whole wheat bread
- 2 slices Cheddar cheese
- 2 slices baked ham
- 2 tablespoons Thousand Island dressing (see page 64)
- 2 tablespoons golden raisins

MIX IT UP: If you don't have a heart-shaped cookie cutter handy, don't worry! Any cookie cutter smaller than a slice of bread will work with this sandwich.

1. Place 2 slices of whole wheat bread on a cutting board. Put 1 slice of Cheddar cheese on each slice of bread.

2. Top each piece of cheese with a slice of ham.

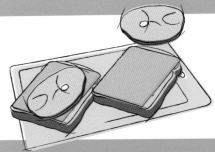

3. Put 1 tablespoon of Thousand Island dressing on top of each slice of ham. Spread it around.

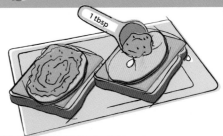

4. Put 1 tablespoon of golden raisins on top of each sandwich.

5. Put a slice of bread on top of each sandwich. Place the cookie cutter on top of the first sandwich and press down to make a heart shape. Repeat with the second sandwich.

Chicken, Peppers, and Shredded Cheddar Cheese in Lettuce Leaf Rolls

TOOLS

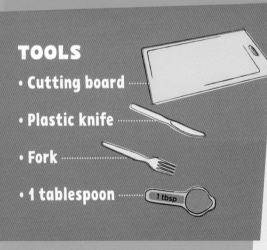

- Cutting board
- Plastic knife
- Fork
- 1 tablespoon

INGREDIENTS

- 1 cooked chicken breast
- ½ red pepper
- 2 large lettuce leaves
- 2 tablespoons shredded Cheddar cheese

GROWN-UP PREP: 1 cooked chicken breast

36

1. On a cutting board, use a plastic knife and fork to cut the cooked chicken breast into thin strips. (If that is too hard, you can also tear it apart using your hands.) Set aside.

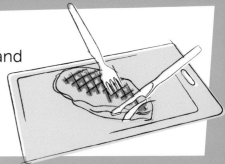

2. On the cutting board, use the plastic knife to cut the red pepper into thin strips. Set aside.

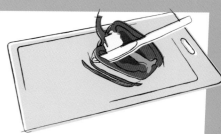

3. Place 2 lettuce leaves on the cutting board. Put half of the chicken in the middle of each leaf.

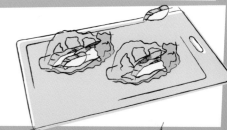

4. Add half of the red pepper strips to each lettuce leaf, laying them in the same direction as the chicken strips.

5. Sprinkle 1 tablespoon of the shredded Cheddar cheese on top of each of the lettuce leaves.

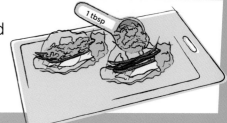

6. Fold or roll the lettuce around the chicken and veggies. The lettuce will be the "bread" in this yummy sandwich.

Pita Pockets with Veggies and Hummus

TOOLS

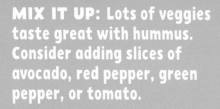

- Cutting board
- Plastic knife
- 1 tablespoon — 1 tbsp

MIX IT UP: Lots of veggies taste great with hummus. Consider adding slices of avocado, red pepper, green pepper, or tomato.

INGREDIENTS

- 1 pita bread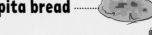
- 1 small cucumber
- 2 lettuce leaves
- 4 tablespoons grated carrot
- 6 tablespoons hummus

GROWN-UP PREP: 4 tablespoons grated carrot

1. On a cutting board, use a plastic knife to cut the pita bread in half. Open up each pita half, trying not to tear the bread. Now you have 2 bread "pockets."

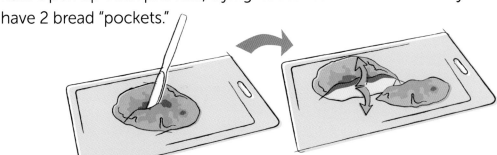

2. On the cutting board, use the plastic knife to thinly slice the cucumber. Place 3 slices of cucumber in each pita pocket. Place a lettuce leaf in each pocket.

3. Add 2 tablespoons of grated carrot to each pita pocket.

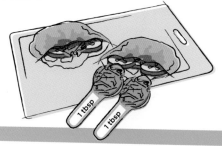

4. Spoon 3 tablespoons of hummus into each pita pocket.

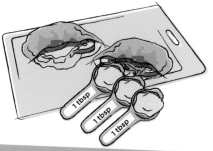

Tuna with Relish and Shredded Carrot in Mini Pitas

TOOLS

- Small bowl
- 1 tablespoon
- Fork
- Cutting board
- Plastic knife

GROWN-UP PREP: 1 can of tuna, opened, drained, and placed in a small bowl; 3 tablespoons grated carrot

INGREDIENTS

- 1 small can tuna
- 2 tablespoons mayonnaise
- 1 tablespoon pickle relish
- 3 mini pita breads
- 3 tablespoons grated carrot

1. Place the bowl of tuna on your work surface. Add 2 tablespoons of mayonnaise to the bowl. Stir together until evenly mixed.

2. Add 1 tablespoon of relish. Stir the mixture.

3. On a cutting board, use a plastic knife to slice 3 mini pitas in half so you end up with 6 small circles.

4. Put 2 tablespoons of the tuna mixture on each of the 3 pita circles and spread it around.

5. Put 1 tablespoon of grated carrot on each sandwich. Top each sandwich with another pita circle.

Roast Beef and Muenster with Mayo and Pickles on Mini Bagels

TOOLS

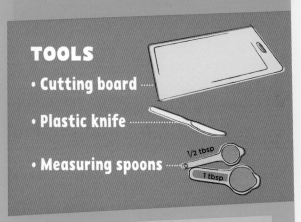

- Cutting board
- Plastic knife
- Measuring spoons

1/2 tbsp
1 tbsp

GROWN-UP PREP: bagels, pre-cut

INGREDIENTS

- **2 mini bagels**
- **2 slices roast beef**
- **2 slices Muenster cheese**
- **1 small pickle**
- **1 tablespoon mayonnaise**

MAYONNAISE

1. Put 2 pre-sliced mini bagels on a cutting board. Place 1 slice of roast beef on each bagel bottom, folding it to fit the bagel shape.

2. Place 1 slice of Muenster cheese on top of the roast beef on each bagel bottom. If you need to, fold the cheese to fit the bagel shape.

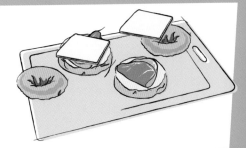

3. On the cutting board, use a plastic knife to cut 6 thin pickle slices. Place 3 pickle slices on top of the cheese on each bagel.

4. Put ½ tablespoon of mayonnaise on top of the pickles on each bagel. Use the plastic knife to spread the mayonnaise around. Place the bagel tops on each sandwich.

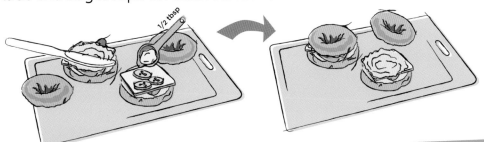

Roast Beef, Swiss, and Pickles in Lettuce Leaf Roll

TOOLS

- Cutting board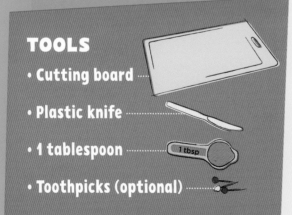
- Plastic knife
- 1 tablespoon
- Toothpicks (optional)

INGREDIENTS

- 1 sour pickle
- 1 big romaine lettuce leaf
- 1 tablespoon Thousand Island dressing (see page 64)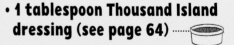
- 1 slice roast beef
- 1 slice Swiss cheese

MIX IT UP: Using lettuce in place of bread is one way to change up your sandwich routine. And it makes many sandwiches gluten-free.

1. On a cutting board, use a plastic knife to cut the pickle in half the long way. Then cut each piece of pickle again the long way so you have 4 long pieces of pickle. Set them aside.

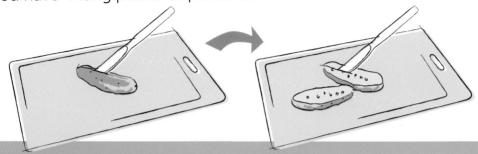

2. Put the lettuce leaf on the cutting board. Add 1 tablespoon of Thousand Island dressing to the lettuce leaf. Use the plastic knife to spread it around.

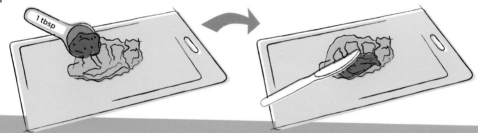

3. Place the pickle slices in the middle of the lettuce leaf. Put the slice of roast beef on top of the pickle slices. Add a slice of Swiss cheese.

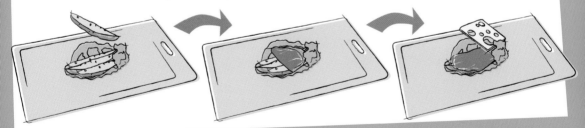

4. Roll the lettuce around the meat, cheese, and pickles. If you like, keep the roll closed with a toothpick.

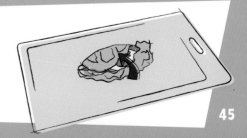

Turkey with Cranberry Sauce and Pear on a Bagel

TOOLS

- Cutting board ....
- 1 tablespoon .... 1 tbsp
- Butter knife ....
- Plastic knife ....

INGREDIENTS

- 1 cinnamon swirl bagel ....
- 3 tablespoons cranberry sauce ....
- 2 slices turkey ....
- ½ ripe pear ....

GROWN-UP PREP: bagel, pre-cut; 1 can of cranberry sauce, opened and placed in a small bowl; pear, washed and cored

1. Place both sides of a pre-sliced bagel on a cutting board. Put 2 tablespoons of cranberry sauce on the bagel bottom. Put 1 tablespoon of cranberry sauce on the bagel top. Use a butter knife to spread the cranberry sauce around on both halves of the bagel.

2. Place 2 turkey slices on top of the cranberry sauce on the bagel bottom.

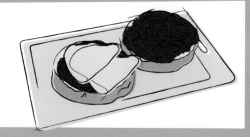

3. On the cutting board, use a plastic knife to thinly slice the cored pear. Lay 3 or 4 slices of pear on top of the turkey. Set the rest of the pear slices to the side.

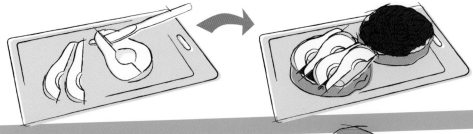

4. Place the bagel top on the pear slices. Eat this bagel sandwich with the rest of the pear slices.

Apple and Peanut Butter Puzzle

TOOLS

- Cutting board
- 1 tablespoon
- Butter knife
- Small plate

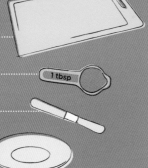

INGREDIENTS

- 1 large apple
- 1 tablespoon lemon juice
- 4–6 tablespoons peanut butter or almond butter

GROWN-UP PREP: apple, cored, horizontally sliced (into 5–7 slices), and brushed with lemon juice to prevent browning

MIX IT UP: As an alternative to peanut or almond butter, use a mixture of honey and oats.

1. For this recipe, you will rebuild the apple using peanut butter between the slices. First, find the slice that was the very bottom of the apple and place it on a cutting board with the cut side up. Put about 1 tablespoon of peanut butter on the apple and use the butter knife to spread it to the edges.

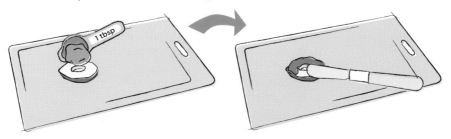

2. Find the next slice up from the bottom. Place it on top of the peanut butter. Put about 1 tablespoon of peanut butter on the apple and use the butter knife to spread it to the edges.

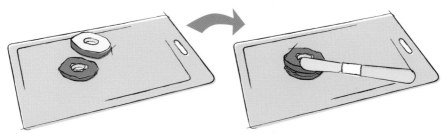

3. Continue rebuilding the apple, spreading peanut butter on each apple slice, until you put the top of the apple in its original place. Move your apple stack to a plate and eat it from the top down!

Dried Fruit and Cereal Snack Mix

TOOLS

- Bowl, container, or resealable bag

- 1 measuring cup
- 1/3 measuring cup
- Wooden spoon

MIX IT UP: Take a small container along on a hike or other outdoor adventure for a quick, crowd-pleasing energy boost.

INGREDIENTS

- 1 cup rice biscuit cereal
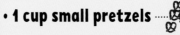
- 1 cup crisped rice cereal

- 1 cup small pretzels
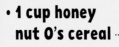
- 1 cup graham cracker cereal

- 1 cup honey nut O's cereal

- 1/3 cup chocolate (or carob) chips

- 1/3 cup dried cranberries

- 1/3 cup golden raisins
- 1/3 cup chopped dates

1. Place a large bowl, container, or bag on your work surface. Add 1 cup rice biscuit cereal, 1 cup crisped rice cereal, 1 cup small pretzels, 1 cup graham cracker cereal, and 1 cup honey nut O's to the bowl.

2. Add 1/3 cup chocolate chips, 1/3 cup dried cranberries, 1/3 cup golden raisins, and 1/3 cup chopped dates. Stir to mix.
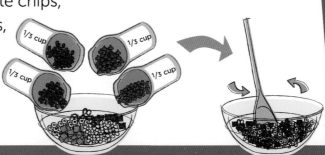

Granola Parfait

TOOLS

- Cutting board
- Plastic knife
- 1 tablespoon
- Parfait or sundae cup

INGREDIENTS

- 2 strawberries
- 1 small container yogurt, any flavor
- 3 tablespoons granola

MIX IT UP: Make this parfait with low-fat yogurt or Greek yogurt. Try it with blueberries, raspberries, or blackberries—or lots of different berries at once. Use bananas and chopped walnuts. Be creative and adventurous!

1. On a cutting board, use a plastic knife to thinly slice the strawberries.

2. Put 3 tablespoons of yogurt into a parfait cup.

TURN PAGE

3. Top with 1 tablespoon of granola.

4. Top the granola with several strawberry slices. That makes the first layer of the parfait.

5. Repeat steps 2 through 4 to make a second layer of the parfait.

6. Then repeat steps 2 through 4 one more time to make a third layer of the parfait. Grab a spoon and enjoy!

Dipped Fruit Slices with Peanut Butter and Cereal, Nuts, Chips, or Sprinkles

TOOLS

- 2 small bowls
- 1/4 measuring cup
- 1 tablespoon
- 4 small plates or a plate with sections
- Cutting board
- Plastic knife
- Butter knife

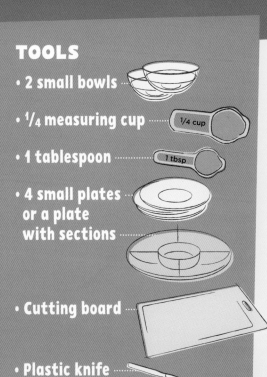

INGREDIENTS

- 1/4 cup peanut butter
- 2 tablespoons lemon juice
- 1/4 cup shredded coconut
- 1/4 cup chocolate chips
- 1/4 cup crisped rice cereal
- 1/4 cup colored sprinkles
- 1 banana
- 1 peach
- 3–4 strawberries

MIX IT UP: Honey or almond butter can be used instead of peanut butter. Granola, chopped walnuts, and raisins are just a few healthy, delicious options for extra toppings.

1. Place 2 small bowls on your work surface. Put 1/4 cup of peanut butter into one bowl. Put 2 tablespoons of lemon juice into the other bowl.

TURN PAGE

CONTINUED
Dipped Fruit Slices with Peanut Butter and Cereal, Nuts, Chips, or Sprinkles

2. Place 4 small plates on your work surface. Put ¼ cup coconut on one plate, ¼ cup chocolate chips on the next plate, ¼ cup crisped rice cereal on the next plate, and ¼ cup sprinkles on the last plate (or add them to different areas of a plate with sections).

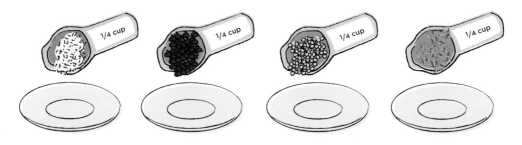

3. Peel the banana. On a cutting board, use a plastic knife to slice it into 4 big pieces. Dip the banana slices in 2 tablespoons of lemon juice and set aside.

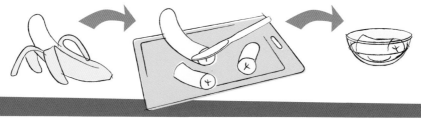

4. Using the plastic knife, slice the peach into big slices. Leave the strawberries whole.

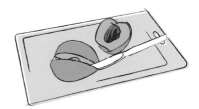

5. Dip a piece of fruit into the peanut butter or spread the peanut butter onto the fruit using the butter knife. When the fruit is covered in peanut butter, roll it in as many toppings as you like. Repeat with the rest of the fruit pieces until they are all covered with toppings. Now, enjoy!

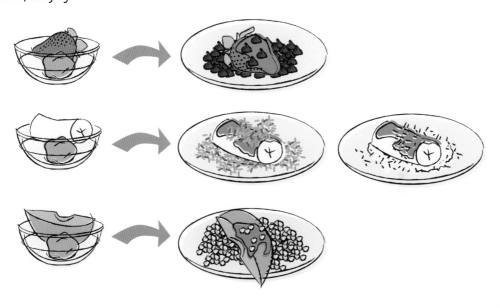

Honey Mustard Dressing

TOOLS

- Medium bowl
- 1 tablespoon
- ¼ measuring cup
- 1 measuring cup
- Wooden spoon

INGREDIENTS

- 3 tablespoons Dijon mustard
- ¼ cup honey
- 1 cup mayonnaise

MIX IT UP: Not a fan of mayonnaise? You can try this recipe with 1 cup of olive oil instead.

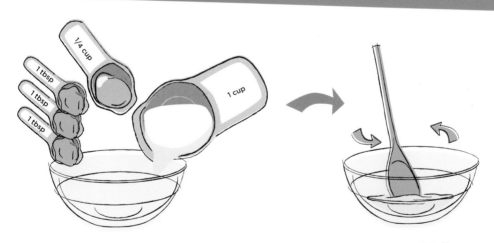

Place a bowl on your work surface. Add 3 tablespoons of Dijon mustard, ¼ cup of honey, and 1 cup of mayonnaise to the bowl. Using a wooden spoon, stir the ingredients together.

Stop

SALADS, DRESSINGS, & DIPS

Vinaigrette Dressing

TOOLS

- **Wide-mouth quart jar with tight-fitting lid**
- **$\frac{1}{3}$ measuring cup**
- **1 tablespoon**
- **1 measuring cup**

INGREDIENTS

- **$\frac{1}{3}$ cup red wine vinegar**
- **2 tablespoons lemon juice**
- **1 tablespoon honey**
- **Salt**
- **Black pepper**
- **1 cup olive oil**

1. Place the jar on your work surface and unscrew the lid. Add ⅓ cup of red wine vinegar and 2 tablespoons of lemon juice to the jar. Then add 1 tablespoon of honey to the jar. Add a pinch of salt and a few grinds of black pepper.

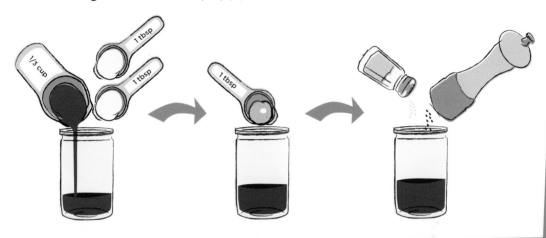

2. Slowly pour 1 cup of olive oil into the jar. Screw on the lid and close tightly. Hold on tight to the jar and shake it for at least 10 seconds. Watch what happens when you set down the dressing after shaking it. The oil and vinegar will separate, and the oil will float to the top. You'll have to shake up the dressing every time you use it.

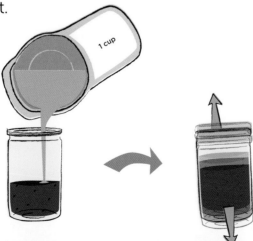

Thousand Island Dressing

TOOLS

- Medium bowl
- 1 measuring cup 1 cup
- 1 tablespoon  1 tbsp
- Wooden spoon

INGREDIENTS

- 1 cup mayonnaise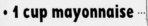
- 5 tablespoons ketchup
- 2 tablespoons pickle relish
- Salt
- Lemon juice

1. Place a bowl on your work surface. Put 1 cup of mayonnaise into the bowl.

2. Add 5 tablespoons of ketchup. Using a wooden spoon, stir until you can't see any white mayonnaise.

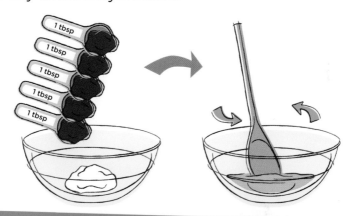

3. Add 2 tablespoons of pickle relish, a pinch of salt, and a few drops of lemon juice. Stir well.

Ranch Dressing

MIX IT UP: Ranch dressing tastes great with veggies like carrots, celery, broccoli, peppers, cucumbers, and cauliflower.

TOOLS

- Medium bowl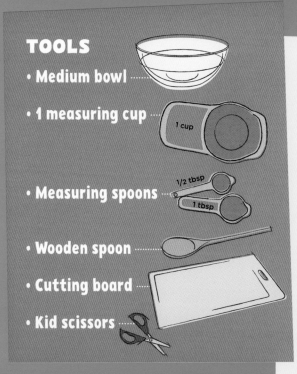
- 1 measuring cup
- Measuring spoons
- Wooden spoon
- Cutting board
- Kid scissors

INGREDIENTS

- 1 cup buttermilk
- 6 tablespoons mayonnaise
- Paprika
- 1 tablespoon lemon juice
- 1/2 tablespoon fresh dill
- 1 tablespoon fresh parsley
- Dry mustard
- Salt

1. Place a bowl on your work surface. Add 1 cup of buttermilk and 6 tablespoons of mayonnaise to the bowl. Using a wooden spoon, mix together well.

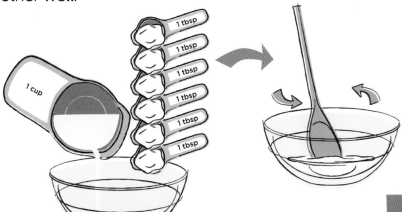

TURN PAGE

2. Add a pinch of paprika and 1 tablespoon of lemon juice. Stir some more.

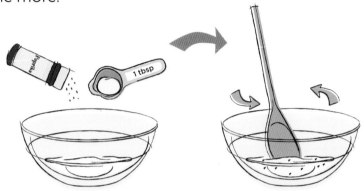

3. Over the cutting board, use the scissors to cut the dill into tiny pieces until you have enough to fill ½ tablespoon. Then cut enough parsley to fill 1 tablespoon.

4. Add ½ tablespoon of dill and 1 tablespoon of parsley to the bowl and mix. Add a pinch of dry mustard and a pinch of salt. Mix well.

Yogurt Salsa Dressing

TOOLS

- Medium bowl ....
- 1 tablespoon ....
- Wooden spoon ....

MIX IT UP: Use less salsa or milder salsa if you do not like spicy foods. Dairy products, such as yogurt or milk, can soothe the sting of spicy foods.

INGREDIENTS

- 1 8-ounce container plain yogurt ....

- 6 tablespoons mild or medium salsa ....

- 1 tablespoon ketchup ....

- Salt ....

70

1. Place a bowl on your work surface. Empty the yogurt container into the bowl.

2. Add 6 tablespoons of salsa to the bowl. Using a wooden spoon, stir to mix.

3. Add 1 tablespoon of ketchup and a pinch of salt. Stir well.

Baby Blue Dressing

MIX IT UP: The blue bits in blue cheese are mold. But don't worry. This mold is safe to eat. It helps give the cheese its creamy texture and tangy flavor. If you don't like blue cheese, try this recipe with feta cheese instead. To make a lighter version of this dressing, use Greek yogurt instead of mayonnaise. If it is too thick, add a tablespoon or two of water.

TOOLS

- Medium bowl
- 1 measuring cup
- Wooden spoon
- Measuring spoons

INGREDIENTS

- 1 cup mayonnaise

- 6 tablespoons blue cheese at room temperature

- 2 tablespoons sour cream

- ½ tablespoon Worcestershire sauce

- ½ tablespoon lemon juice

- Salt

- Garlic powder

- Dry mustard

- Black pepper

1. Place a bowl on your work surface. Put 1 cup of mayonnaise into the bowl. Using a wooden spoon, stir until it looks smooth.

TURN PAGE

2. Add 6 tablespoons of blue cheese and stir again. (Room-temperature blue cheese should mix easily. If it doesn't, use your fingers to crumble the cheese.)

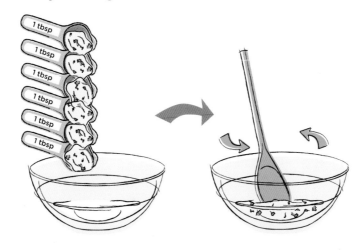

3. Add 2 tablespoons of sour cream and stir until it is well mixed.

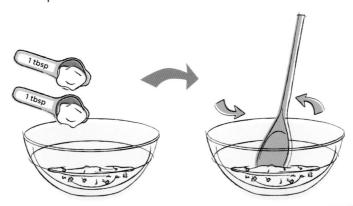

4. Add ½ tablespoon of Worcestershire sauce and ½ tablespoon of lemon juice to the bowl and stir again.

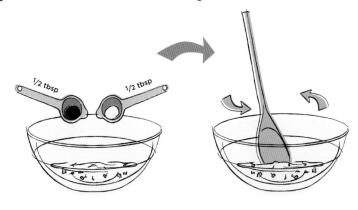

5. Add a pinch of salt, a pinch of garlic powder, a pinch of dry mustard, and a few grinds of black pepper. Stir until the dressing is well mixed.

Chopped Salad
SERVES 4

TOOLS

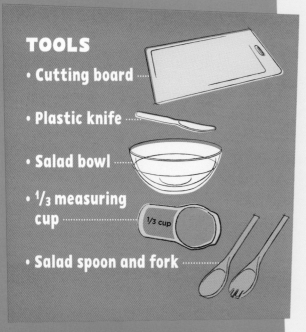

- Cutting board
- Plastic knife
- Salad bowl
- 1/3 measuring cup
- Salad spoon and fork

INGREDIENTS

- 1 head romaine lettuce
- ½ cucumber
- 1 tomato
- ½ red pepper
- 4 slices baked turkey
- 4 slices roast ham
- 4 slices Swiss cheese
- 1/3 cup of your favorite dressing

1. Place a head of lettuce on a cutting board. Use your hands to pull the lettuce leaves from the head.

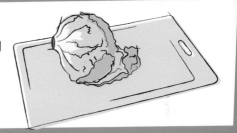

2. Using the plastic knife, chop the leaves into small, bite-size pieces. Put the chopped lettuce into the bowl.

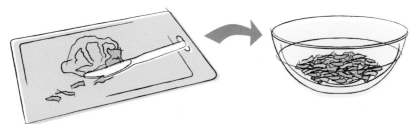

TURN PAGE

3. On the cutting board, use the plastic knife to cut the cucumber into thin slices. Then cut each cucumber slice into 4 pieces. Add the pieces to the bowl.

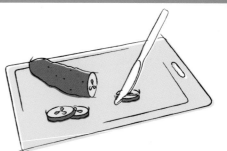

4. Use the plastic knife to cut the tomato and the red pepper into small pieces. Add the pieces to the bowl.

5. Cut the turkey, ham, and Swiss cheese into small pieces. Add the pieces to the bowl.

6. Pour ⅓ cup of dressing over the salad. Using a salad spoon and fork, mix well. If you like more dressing, add another 1 or 2 tablespoons of dressing.

MIX IT UP: A colorful plate is a healthy plate because different colored foods contain different nutrients. Swap red peppers and tomatoes for yellow, orange, or green varieties. Try out red or purple lettuces. Can you taste the difference between a red and green pepper? Red and green lettuce?

Fried Chicken Salad
SERVES 4

TOOLS

- Cutting board
- Plastic knife
- Fork
- Large bowl
- 1 measuring cup
- 1/2 measuring cup
- 1/3 measuring cup
- Wooden spoons

INGREDIENTS

- 2 boneless, fried chicken breasts
- 1 head lettuce or small bag mixed greens
- 1 cup cherry tomatoes
- 1/2 cup shredded Cheddar cheese
- 1/3 cup baby blue dressing (see page 72)

1. On a cutting board, use a plastic knife and fork to cut the chicken into bite-size pieces. Put the chicken into a bowl on your work surface.

2. Using your hands, tear the head of lettuce into bite-size pieces and add them to the bowl.

3. On the cutting board, use the plastic knife to cut 1 cup of cherry tomatoes in half. Add them to the bowl.

4. Add ½ cup of Cheddar cheese and ⅓ cup of baby blue dressing to the bowl. Using wooden spoons, mix well.

 **SALADS, DRESSINGS, & DIPS**

Pasta Salad with Cheese, Tomato, and Pesto

SERVES 4

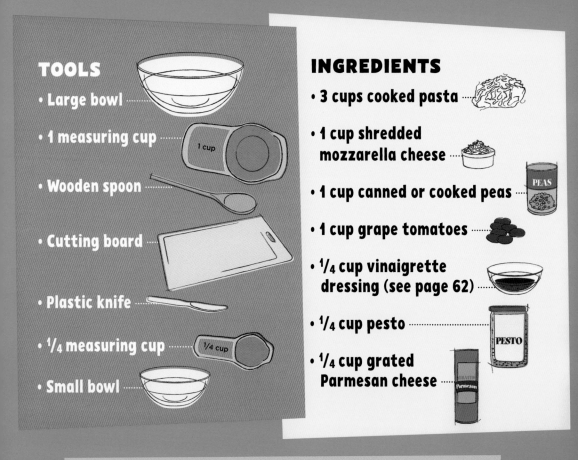

TOOLS

- Large bowl
- 1 measuring cup
- Wooden spoon
- Cutting board
- Plastic knife
- ¼ measuring cup
- Small bowl

INGREDIENTS

- 3 cups cooked pasta
- 1 cup shredded mozzarella cheese
- 1 cup canned or cooked peas
- 1 cup grape tomatoes
- ¼ cup vinaigrette dressing (see page 62)
- ¼ cup pesto
- ¼ cup grated Parmesan cheese

GROWN-UP PREP: pasta, cooked, drained, and cooled; fresh peas, cooked, drained, and cooled, or canned peas, opened, drained, and put into a bowl

1. Place a large bowl on your work surface. Put the cooked pasta into the bowl.

TURN PAGE

2. Add 1 cup of shredded mozzarella cheese and 1 cup of peas to the bowl. Using a wooden spoon, mix well.

3. On a cutting board, use a plastic knife to cut 1 cup of grape tomatoes in half. Add them to the bowl.

4. Put ¼ cup vinaigrette and ¼ cup pesto into a small bowl. Use a wooden spoon to mix well.

5. Pour ¼ cup of the vinaigrette and pesto mixture over the pasta mixture. Sprinkle with ¼ cup of grated Parmesan cheese and serve.

MIX IT UP: Pesto means something that is ground into a paste. Usually the ingredients that are ground up are basil, garlic, pine nuts, parmesan cheese, and olive oil. Some people use different herbs (such as parsley) instead of basil. And some people use walnuts, almonds, or other nuts instead of pine nuts. You can use different kinds of pesto in this delightful salad.

Rice Salad with Raisins, Berries, and Other Good Stuff SERVES 4

TOOLS

- Large bowl
- ¼ measuring cup
- 1 tablespoon
- Wooden spoon
- Cutting board
- Plastic knife

INGREDIENTS

- 3 cups cooked jasmine brown rice (or couscous)
- ¼ cup golden raisins
- 2 tablespoons dried cranberries
- 2 tablespoons chopped dried apricots
- 8 strawberries
- 8 seedless grapes
- ¼ cup vinaigrette dressing (see page 62)

GROWN-UP PREP: rice or couscous, cooked

1. Place a large bowl on your work surface. Put the cooked rice (or couscous) into the bowl.

2. Add ¼ cup of golden raisins, 2 tablespoons of dried cranberries, and 2 tablespoons of chopped dried apricots to the bowl. Use a wooden spoon to mix.

3. On a cutting board, use a plastic knife to slice the strawberries thinly. Add the strawberry slices to the bowl.

4. Cut the grapes in half. Add the grape halves to the bowl. Stir to mix.

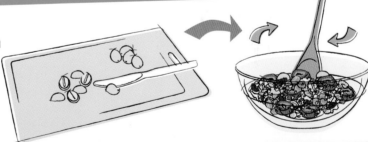

5. Add ¼ cup of vinaigrette to the rice or couscous mixture. Using the wooden spoon, stir gently to combine.

Sesame Noodle Salad
SERVES 4

TOOLS

- Medium bowl
- ½ measuring cup
- ¼ measuring cup
- Wooden spoon
- Measuring spoons
- Cutting board
- Plastic knife
- Large bowl

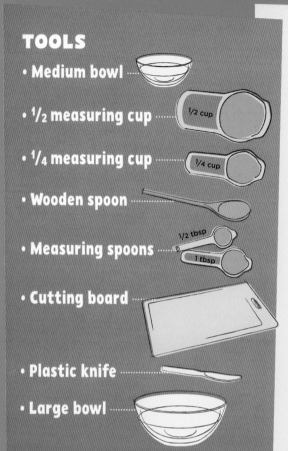

INGREDIENTS

- ½ cup smooth peanut butter
- ¼ cup soy sauce
- 2 tablespoons red wine vinegar
- 1½ tablespoons Asian sesame oil
- 1 tablespoon honey
- 3 pepper halves
- 1 pound cooked linguine or spaghetti noodles

GROWN-UP PREP: noodles, cooked, drained, and cooled

1. Place a medium bowl on your work surface. Add ½ cup of peanut butter and ¼ cup of soy sauce to the bowl. Using a wooden spoon, stir well.

TURN PAGE

2. Add 5 tablespoons of warm water to the peanut butter mixture and stir again.

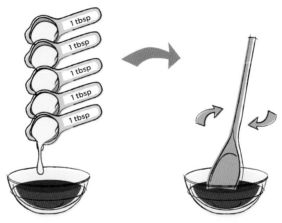

3. Add 2 tablespoons of red wine vinegar, 1½ tablespoons of sesame oil, and 1 tablespoon of honey. Stir to mix.

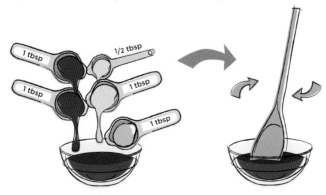

4. On a cutting board, use a plastic knife to cut the peppers into very thin strips.

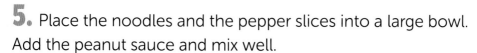

5. Place the noodles and the pepper slices into a large bowl. Add the peanut sauce and mix well.

MIX IT UP: If you have it, use unsalted peanut butter for this recipe. Try whole wheat noodles as well. Be sure to refrigerate any leftovers—this salad tastes great cold!

Triple Bean Salad
SERVES 4

TOOLS

- 5 small bowls
- Large bowl
- 1 measuring cup
- Wooden spoons
- Kid scissors
- Cutting board
- Plastic knife
- 1 tablespoon
- ½ measuring cup

INGREDIENTS

- 1 cup garbanzo beans
- 1 cup canned or cooked corn
- 1 cup light red kidney beans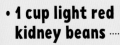
- 1 cup black beans
- ½ bunch cilantro or parsley
- ½ avocado
- 1 tablespoon lemon juice
- ½ cup of vinaigrette dressing (see page 62)

GROWN-UP PREP: 3 types of beans and 1 can of corn, each opened and drained into separate bowls; 1 avocado, pitted and peeled

1. Place a large bowl on your work surface. Put 1 cup garbanzo beans, 1 cup corn, 1 cup kidney beans, and 1 cup black beans into the bowl. Using a wooden spoon, stir to mix.

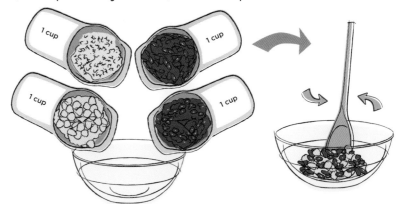

2. Over the bowl, use scissors to snip the cilantro or parsley into very small pieces.

3. On a cutting board, use a plastic knife to cut the avocado into small chunks. Place the avocado into a small bowl. Add 1 tablespoon of lemon juice and mix well. (The lemon juice will keep the avocado from turning brown.)

4. Add the avocado to the bean mixture. Add ½ cup of vinaigrette dressing and mix well.

Corn Salad
SERVES 4

TOOLS

- Cutting board
- Plastic knife
- Large bowl
- Wooden spoon
- 1 tablespoon

INGREDIENTS
- ½ orange pepper
- ½ red pepper
- 1 ripe tomato
- 1 16-ounce package frozen corn
- 5 tablespoons yogurt salsa dressing (see page 70)

GROWN-UP PREP: frozen corn, thawed and drained

94

1. On a cutting board, use a plastic knife to cut the peppers into small pieces. Place a large bowl on your work surface. Put the pepper pieces into the bowl.

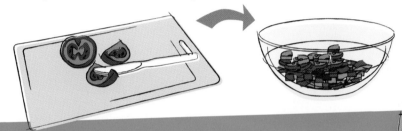

2. On the cutting board, use the plastic knife to cut the tomato into small pieces. Add tomato pieces to the bowl.

3. Put the corn into the bowl. Using a wooden spoon, stir ingredients together.

4. Add 5 tablespoons of the yogurt salsa dressing and stir until well mixed.

1 tbsp
1 tbsp
1 tbsp
1 tbsp
1 tbsp

Potato Salad
SERVES 4

TOOLS

- Large bowl
- Kid scissors
- 1 tablespoon
- Cutting board
- Plastic knife
- 1 measuring cup
- Wooden spoon

INGREDIENTS

- 2 tablespoons fresh dill
- 3 cups cooked potatoes
- 1 cup canned or cooked peas
- Salt
- Pepper
- 6 tablespoons Thousand Island dressing (see page 64)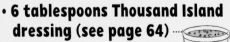

1. Place a bowl on your work surface. Over the bowl, use scissors to finely cut up about 2 tablespoons of dill.

2. On a cutting board, use a plastic knife to cut the potatoes into bite-size chunks. Add them to the bowl.

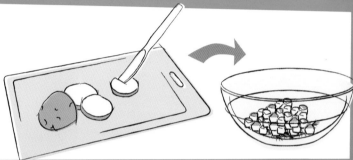

3. Add 1 cup of peas to the bowl. Add a pinch of salt and a few grinds of pepper. Using a wooden spoon, stir ingredients together.

4. Add 6 tablespoons of Thousand Island dressing to the bowl. Using a wooden spoon, stir ingredients together.

Frozen Honey-Dipped Bananas
SERVES 2

TOOLS

- Cutting board
- Plastic knife
- Wax paper
- Baking sheet
- 1 tablespoon
- 4 wooden pop sticks
- Resealable bag
- 3 small plates
- 1 measuring cup

INGREDIENTS

- 2 bananas
- 3 tablespoons lemon juice
- Honey
- 1 cup colored sprinkles
- 1 cup crisped rice cereal

MIX IT UP: If you don't have much time or want to cut down on sugar, frozen banana pops are delicious without any toppings. They taste like banana ice cream!

1. Peel the bananas. On a cutting board, use a plastic knife to cut them in half crosswise.

2. Place a piece of wax paper on a baking sheet. Put 3 tablespoons of lemon juice on the wax paper and roll the banana pieces in the lemon juice.

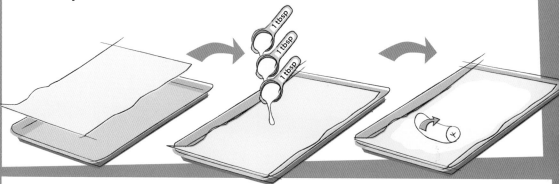

3. Stick a wooden pop stick into the bottom of each banana piece. Place the bananas in a bag or container and put them in the freezer until frozen.

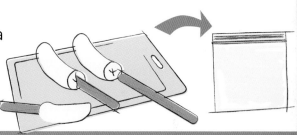

4. When you're ready to eat the banana pops, take them out of the freezer. Squeeze some honey onto a plate. Pour 1 cup of sprinkles on another plate and 1 cup of cereal on a third plate. Twirl a banana piece in the honey, covering it as much as you can. Then, roll the banana in sprinkles, cereal, or both. Repeat with each banana pop.

Fresh Fruit and Yogurt Cones

TOOLS

- Cutting board
- Plastic knife
- 1 tablespoon

INGREDIENTS

- 2 strawberries
- 1 flat-bottom ice cream cone
- 6 raspberries
- 6 blueberries
- 2 tablespoons flavored yogurt

MIX IT UP: Experiment with different fruit combos for this treat. Try sliced nectarines, plums, and apricots or blackberries, peaches, and honeydew melon.

1. On a cutting board, use a plastic knife to thinly slice the strawberries.

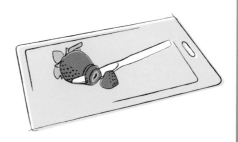

2. Put the ice cream cone on the cutting board and fill it with the strawberry slices, raspberries, and blueberries.

3. Drizzle 2 tablespoons of yogurt on top of the fruit.

DESSERTS

Ice Cream Cookie Sandwiches with Sprinkles SERVES 4

TOOLS

- Cutting board

- Ice cream scoop

- ½ measuring cup

- Small plate

INGREDIENTS

- 1 pint ice cream or frozen yogurt, any flavor

- 8 cookies, any flavor

- ½ cup chocolate or colored sprinkles

MIX IT UP: A few hours before making these ice cream sandwiches, chop pineapples or strawberries into tiny pieces and freeze them. These frozen fruit bits are packed with flavor and are a nice alternative to sprinkles. For a savory swap, use crushed pretzel pieces instead.

1. Take the ice cream out of the freezer and let it soften for about 10 minutes.

2. Place 4 cookies on your cutting board, with the flat side facing up. As soon as the ice cream is soft enough, put 1 scoop of ice cream on each cookie.

3. Place a cookie on top of each ice cream scoop. Press down gently.

4. Put ½ cup of sprinkles on a plate. Roll the edges of the cookies in the sprinkles. Place the cookies back in the freezer until they freeze again, about 20 minutes.

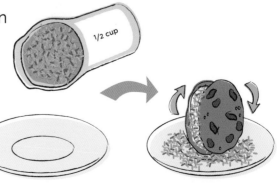

Indoor S'mores

SERVES 2

TOOLS

- Cutting board
- 1 tablespoon
- Butter knife

INGREDIENTS

- 4 double graham crackers
- 4 tablespoons chocolate frosting
- 4 tablespoons marshmallow creme

MIX IT UP: Indoors, eat these extra-sweet treats by a warm fire while telling spooky stories. On a warm summer night, eat them outside under the stars.

1. Over a cutting board, break 4 double graham crackers in half along the scored line. Now you have 8 square crackers.

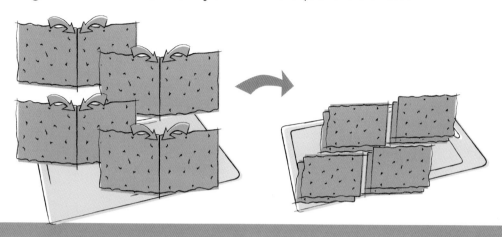

2. Put 1 tablespoon of frosting onto each of 4 graham cracker halves. Using a butter knife, spread the frosting around.

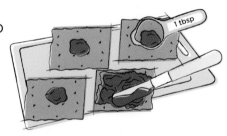

3. Put 1 tablespoon of marshmallow creme onto each of the 4 remaining crackers. Using a butter knife, spread the creme around.

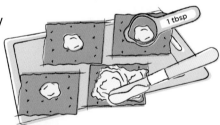

4. Put the crackers together so the chocolate frosting is pressed against the marshmallow creme.

Strawberry Tall Cake SERVES 4

TOOLS

- Cutting board

- Plastic knife

- Medium bowl

- Rectangular platter

- 1 tablespoon

INGREDIENTS

- 12 large strawberries

- 1 frozen pound cake, defrosted

- 10 tablespoons strawberry syrup

- 1 can whipped cream

GROWN-UP PREP: pound cake, defrosted and sliced horizontally into 3 equal pieces

1. On a cutting board, use a plastic knife to thinly slice 11 strawberries. (Save 1 whole strawberry.) Place a medium bowl on your work surface. Put the strawberry slices in the bowl.

2. Place the platter on your work surface. Put the bottom slice of cake on the platter. Spread about half of the strawberries over the cake slice.

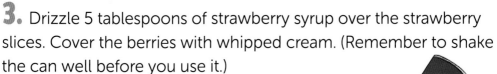

3. Drizzle 5 tablespoons of strawberry syrup over the strawberry slices. Cover the berries with whipped cream. (Remember to shake the can well before you use it.)

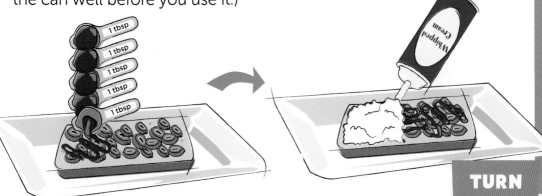

TURN PAGE

4. To make the second layer, place another slice of cake on top of the whipped cream. Put a little more than half of the remaining strawberry slices on the cake.

5. Drizzle with 5 tablespoons of strawberry syrup. Cover the second layer of berries in whipped cream.

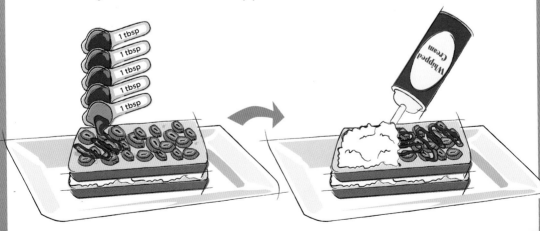

6. Place the last slice of the pound cake on top of the layered cake. Put the remaining strawberry slices on top.

7. Place 1 whole berry on top of the cake.

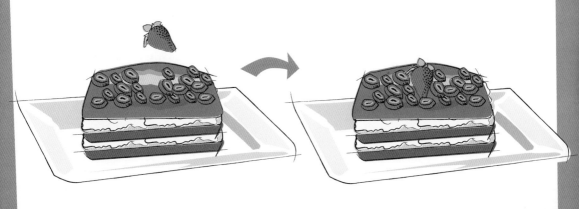

MIX IT UP: For a lighter dessert, substitute yogurt loaf cake for the pound cake and cream cheese or cottage cheese for the whipped cream. To use cream cheese, make sure it is room temperature and spread it on each layer before adding the strawberries.

Tiny Trifle SERVES 4

TOOLS

- Resealable bag

- 4 custard cups or ramekins

- 1 tablespoon

- Medium bowl

- 1 measuring cup

- Hand mixer

INGREDIENTS

- 16 vanilla wafers

- 32 raspberries

- 8 tablespoons chocolate syrup

- 1 small package instant vanilla pudding mix

- 2 cups 2% milk

1. Put 16 vanilla wafers into the resealable bag and close it securely. Press down on the cookies in the bag to break them into chunks. DO NOT turn them into crumbs! There should be some big pieces.

2. Place 4 custard cups on your work surface. Put 2 tablespoons of the cookie pieces in the bottom of each cup. Set aside any extra cookie pieces.

MIX IT UP: A trifle is a cold dessert, often made of cake and fruit covered with jelly, custard, and cream. Trifles are a popular dessert in England. In your trifle, try using raspberry jam instead of chocolate syrup.

TURN PAGE

3. Place 4 raspberries into each custard cup.

4. Drizzle 1 tablespoon of chocolate syrup into each custard cup.

5. Make the instant pudding by mixing the milk with the pudding powder and using the mixer to beat the pudding until it is completely smooth.

6. Put equal amounts of pudding into each of the 4 cups. Then put the cups in the refrigerator for about 10 minutes. Use a timer or sing 3 or 4 different songs while you wait.

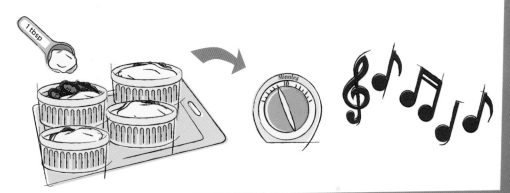

7. Take the cups out of the fridge. Add 4 raspberries to each cup. Sprinkle each cup with some of the cookie pieces and top each cup with 1 tablespoon of chocolate syrup.

 **DRINKS**

Egg Cream

TOOLS

- **Tall drinking glass** ⋯⋯⋯⋯
- **¹/₂ measuring cup** ⋯⋯
- **1 measuring cup** ⋯⋯
- **1 tablespoon** ⋯⋯⋯⋯
- **Wooden spoon** ⋯⋯⋯

MIX IT UP: It's fine to use 1% or 2% milk rather than whole milk.

INGREDIENTS

- **¹/₂ cup whole milk** ⋯⋯
- **1 cup cold seltzer** ⋯⋯
- **2 tablespoons chocolate syrup** ⋯⋯

1. Place a tall glass on your work surface. Pour ½ cup of milk into the glass.

2. Pour 1 cup of seltzer into the glass.

3. Add 2 tablespoons of chocolate syrup and stir with a wooden spoon to mix. **NOTE:** Drink within 5 minutes or the fizz will be gone.

DRINKS

Orange Juice
Strawberry Spritzer

TOOLS

- Tall drinking glass ....
- 1 measuring cup ....
- Cutting board ....
- Plastic knife ....
- 1 tablespoon ....
- Wooden spoon ....

MIX IT UP: Orange juice isn't the only juice that tastes great with bubbles. Add seltzer to grape juice, grapefuit juice, pineapple juice, or cranberry juice for more fizzy fun.

INGREDIENTS

- 1 cup orange juice ....
- 2 strawberries ....
- 4 tablespoons seltzer ....

1. Place a tall glass on your work surface. Add 1 cup of orange juice. Set the glass aside.

2. On a cutting board, use a plastic knife to cut the strawberries into thin slices.

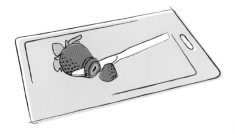

3. Add the strawberry slices to the juice. Just before drinking, add 4 tablespoons of seltzer. Stir and enjoy.

 **DRINKS**

Fruity Ice Cubes

TOOLS

- Measuring cup with spout

- Ice cube tray

MIX IT UP: Instead of raspberries, use blueberries or chopped-up cucumbers. Basil is a tasty alternative to mint. Find the fruit and herb combo you like best!

INGREDIENTS

- Water

- 24 raspberries

- 12 mint leaves

1. Using the measuring cup with a spout, fill each section of an ice cube tray half full with water.

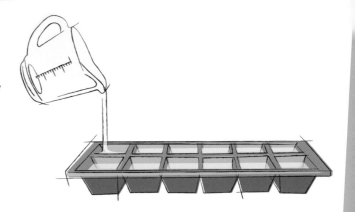

2. Put 2 raspberries and 1 mint leaf in each section. Place the ice cube tray in the freezer for 30 minutes. Use a timer or watch an episode of one of your favorite cartoons.

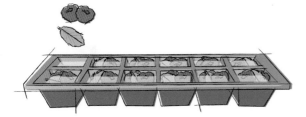

3. Remove the tray from the freezer. Fill the sections, covering the fruit with water. Freeze again until solid. When you are ready for a pretty, refreshing drink, add a few ice cubes to a cup. Then fill it up with water, seltzer, or lemonade.

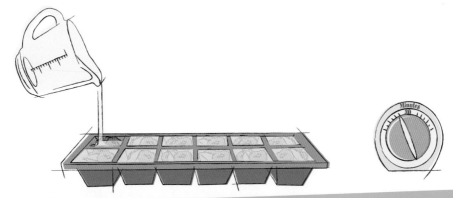

Party Punch
SERVES 4–6

MIX IT UP: Experiment with flavors to find the combination of juices you like best. Swap in cranberry juice for white grape juice or ginger ale for pineapple juice. You can also serve your Party Punch with Fruity Ice Cubes (see page 118).

TOOLS

- Large plastic pitcher
- 1 measuring cup
- Cutting board
- Plastic knife
- Wooden spoon

INGREDIENTS

- 3 cups orange juice
- 1 cup pink lemonade
- 1 cup white grape juice
- 1 cup pineapple juice
- 12 strawberries
- 24 raspberries
- 1 peach

1. Place a large plastic pitcher on your work surface. Pour 3 cups of orange juice into the pitcher.

TURN PAGE

CONTINUED Party Punch

2. Pour 1 cup of pink lemonade, 1 cup of white grape juice, and 1 cup of pineapple juice into the pitcher. Set aside.

3. On a cutting board, use a plastic knife to cut the strawberries into thin slices.

4. Put the strawberry slices into the pitcher. Add the 24 raspberries to the pitcher as well.

5. On the cutting board, use the plastic knife to slice the peach in half. Twist the two halves to separate. Remove the pit and throw it away. Cut each peach half into thin slices.

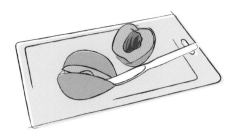

6. Add the peach slices to the pitcher. Using a wooden spoon, stir until everything is mixed well.

Raspberry Lemonade
SERVES 4–6

TOOLS

- Large plastic pitcher
- 1 measuring cup
- Wooden spoon
- Medium bowl

INGREDIENTS

- 1 cup super fine sugar
- 1 cup lemon juice
- 4 cups water
- 20 fresh raspberries

MIX IT UP: Try sweetening your lemonade with honey. If you like your lemonade to be tart, use less sugar.

1. Place a large plastic pitcher on your work surface. Add 1 cup of super fine sugar and 1 cup of lemon juice to the pitcher. Using a wooden spoon, stir to dissolve the sugar.

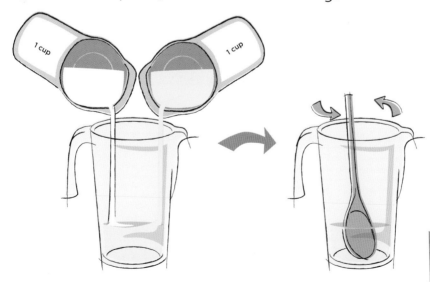

TURN PAGE

2. Add 4 cups of water to the pitcher and stir again.

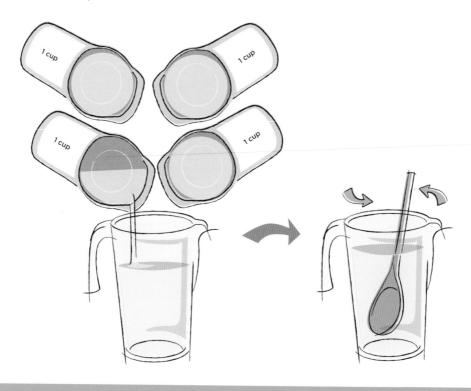

3. Place a medium bowl on your work surface. Put the raspberries into the bowl and mash them with the wooden spoon. (They do not need to be completely squished.)

4. Add the raspberries to the pitcher and stir with the wooden spoon.

INDEX BY KEY INGREDIENT

If you've got leftover rice or too many crackers, or if you have a craving for bananas, this will steer you to the right recipe.